The Trouble with Teachers

D0802524

Based on the TV series *Angela Anaconda*®
created by Joanna Ferrone and Sue Rose as seen on the Fox Family Channel®

SIMON SPOTLIGHT
An imprint of Simon & Schuster Children's Publishing Division
1230 Avenue of the Americas, New York, New York 10020

Manufactured in the United States of America

First Edition
4 6 8 10 9 7 5 3

ISBN 0-689-83996-0

Library of Congress Control Number 00-107899

THE TROUBLE WITH
TEACHERS

adapted by Barbara Calamari

based on the scripts by
Rachelle Romberg

illustrated by Elizabeth Brandt

Simon Spotlight

New York　　London　　Toronto　　Sydney　　Singapore

Story Number One

You're So Vain

CHAPTER ONE

Hello, in case you don't know this already, my name is Angela Anaconda, and I want to tell you about something terrible that happened to me in school one day that was not my fault. At all. It was just another boring day in my third-grade classroom at Tapwater Springs Elementary. Mrs. Brinks, our teacher, who is mean to everyone except Miss Teacher's Pet, Ninnie Wart Manoir (otherwise known as Nanette), told us we had to write a rhyming poem about someone we really admire. Of course, Nanette wanted to know if we could put French words in our poems. Why, you ask? Because Nanette Manoir, who is *not* French, wants everybody to think she *is* French, even though she is *not*. And since Mrs. Brinks has never said the word "NO" (which rhymes with THROW, as in throw up), Nanette is allowed to use French in her poem. But who cares, because how was I supposed to know this was the assignment that was about to ruin my whole life?

On the way home from school that day, with my best friends Gina Lash and Johnny Abatti, I thought of everybody who was important to me. Then Gina Lash said, "You'll never guess my pick, Angela Anaconda. It's Tiny Dottie, the snack food czar. She's a successful entrepreneur and she makes a darn good cream cake. Just think of

the research *I'll* get to do!"

You see, Gina Lash loves to eat, and what she loves to eat the most is Tiny Dottie cakes, especially those pink coconut snowballs. She can eat fourteen in one day. But what I would like to know is, how come Tiny Dottie is so tiny if her cakes are so darn good?

Then Johnny Abatti says he is going to write about his uncle Nicky. "He's the best! He hardly ever went to school, and he never goes to work, and he drives real fast, too!"

"Of course he does," says Gina Lash. "That's because he's always being chased by the police." So, anyway, then it is my turn to share, and I tell my friends they are just going to have to guess who I'm picking because I am not telling. And even Gina Lash, the smartest in class, can't guess.

"Why don't you just tell us?" she and Johnny ask me.

"Because it's a secret," I tell them. "And if I tell, it won't be a secret anymore. Even *I* know that."

"But we told you who we admire most."

"Sorry, Johnny and Gina," I tell them. "A surprise is a surprise on account of it's a surprise." And then we got to my house where I live and I waved good-bye to my friends. "See you later when you see me!" I tell them.

Like I said, Johnny and Gina are my best friends except for one friend who's an even *better* best friend—the best friend anybody could ever have! Can you guess who that is? It's who comes to greet me on my front walk and almost knocks me over and licks my face every day: my pet dog, King!

"Hello, King," I say. "How's my girl, the best dog in the entire world?" And when we run into the house I cannot wait to tell King all about my new assignment. "We have to write a poem about someone we admire enough to write a poem about, and nobody picked as good a pick as mine!" I tell her.

So, we walk into the kitchen, and there's my mom: "Hi, sweetie, I made chocolate chips, but no cookies till you wash your hands," she tells me, even though they look perfectly clean to me and I don't get or see how cookies could make my hands dirty. "Oh, brother," I say to myself, except whenever I say something to myself, my mother can always seem to hear it from ten miles away. See, my mom might be really nice for a mother, and I like her a lot and wouldn't want a different one, but sometimes she drives me crazy.

"March!" she tells me.

While I'm in the bathroom washing my hands, I tell King all about my project.

"The someone I am writing about looks out for everyone in my family, and when I grow up, I want to be just like her!" I explain. Then I notice that King must be thirsty, because she's doing something truly gross: she's drinking from the toilet bowl. "Well, except for the drinking from the toilet thing," I tell her. "Can you guess who it is, girl?" Because she is so smart, King answers with a bark. "You're right. It's you, King!"

So that night I work very hard on writing my poem, and I cannot wait to get to school tomorrow.

CHAPTER TWO

The next day at school Johnny and Gina can't wait to know who I picked, but I still will not tell them. Josephine Praline, who loves religion, goes first, and she wrote a poem about a nun who was burned at the stake. *That* made everyone quiet. Then Mrs. Big Mouth Brinks gets up and asks her favorite pet, Nanette Manoir, to go next. I can see Johnny and Gina turn red. They know for sure that Nanette Manoir is not

going to stop talking for ten hours at least and they want to know who I picked and this will make them have to wait.

When Miss Nanny-goat herself stands up, there is a lot of oohing and aahing from her Copycat-Clone-Club, January and Karlene. "Why, Nanette," says Mrs. Brinks (like she was in love), "what a pretty new frock you have on!"

"*Merci beaucoup*, Mrs. Brinks," says creepy Nin. "It's a Paris original in honor of the person I have chosen for my poem: Marie Antoinette, the famous queen of France." Not only does Nanette have a superfancy shiny dress on, she also has a giant picture of that queen who wanted everyone to eat cake so they cut her head off.

Anyway, Nanette starts torturing us with her poem, when a miracle happens and Nanumbskull sits back down again! "I'm sorry, Mrs. Brinks," she says, "but I was planning to use the recess period to perfect the delivery of my lengthy poem about royalty. Perhaps Angela, who undoubtedly has written something substantially shorter, should go first."

Then those clone drone friends of hers, January and Karlene, start to laugh, and since Mrs. Brinks always agrees with everything that comes out of Nanette Manoir's un-French mouth, she says, "How considerate of you, Nanette!"

Then it was a dream come true for Johnny and Gina. Mrs. Brinks tells me to stand up and read my poem first.

CHAPTER THREE

Before beginning I decided to say a few words as an introduction: "Even though some kids picked someone *famous* to write about, I decided to write about someone I truly admire. Someone I learn from every day." All of a sudden even Mrs. Brinks is interested. "Okay, here goes," I say. Since I'm never used to all that attention, I then clear my throat and begin:

"You have perfect manners,
You never drool.

You even help me get through school.
You're playful and friendly,
You're open and brave.
It's you who teaches me how to behave.
In the garden beds where you usually go,
It seems to help the flowers grow.
Even your little whiskers are neat
And the fuzzy fur upon your feet.
Your hair is so beautiful,
You don't need to wear clothes,
You're devoted and loyal,
And I like your cold, wet nose.
You're the very best role model I've ever met.
It is I who should be *your* pet. The end."

In my entire year in this classroom I have never done as well as now! Mrs. Brinks is actually crying! At first I think it is because I said something wrong, but the real reason is that she is so happy. "Miss Anaconda, I never knew," she said. "You have the makings of the next Emily Dickinson!"

(Whoever *that* is.)

Even though Johnny and Gina look a little annoyed, I figure it is because they are so jealous. And if Ninnie Wart's brain was not so damp and soggy, there would have been steam coming out of her ears. "Don't worry, Nanette," says her clone friend January, "I'm sure your poem is much better than hers."

And by the look on Dim Nin's face, I can tell it is not.

Up until that point I am the happiest I will ever be in that class. Then Mrs. Brinks says something that ruins everything. "Well, Miss Anaconda, you could've knocked me down with a feather. I had no idea you felt this way about me!"

What did she say? All of a sudden everything that was so good is now so bad. I try to tell Mrs. Brinks that the poem is really about King and definitely not about her, but I can't speak and she keeps making things worse by getting happier and happier. Then she decides that she wants me to write my poem out on the blackboard for the whole school to see. Things get more terrible when Nanette and her dumb duet are leaving for recess and I'm still stuck writing on the board.

"At least I'm not a brownnoser like Angela Anaconda," says Nanette. *"Your beautiful hair, your lovely gaze. Since I wrote this poem, I get straight A's."*

You know what the worst part is? Even if I did write that poem about Mrs. Brinks like everyone thought I did, then I would hate me even more than Nanette does.

CHAPTER FOUR

Out on the playground that day it's terrible. Johnny Abatti and Gina Lash act like they hardly even know me. All the other kids are whispering about me. Finally I catch up to Johnny and Gina on the swings and Johnny is so surprised, he can't keep quiet any longer. "Mrs. Brinks? Since when did you start liking *her*?" he asks.

"Come on, Johnny and Gina," I tell them. "You know I wouldn't write a poem like that about Mrs. Brinks. I wrote it about KING!"

Both of them get very confused.

"As in Martin Luther King?" asks Gina.

"Or Elvis?" asks Johnny.

"Not THE King," I say. "My dog King!" At first I didn't think either one of them really believed me. "I knew I should've left in that part about 'drinking from the toilet.'"

Then Gina Lash finally looks in my face, which was very upset, and says, "Angela Anaconda, you are really in a pickle."

"I tried to tell Mrs. Brinks," I explain. Then Gina says never, ever, under any circumstance tell Mrs. Brinks. And she doesn't even have to tell me that on account of I know how mad Mrs. Brinks would get at me if she found out that poem was really written about my dog.

Then creepy Karlene comes over and says,

"Look, it's Angela Ana-buttkisser." And then her creepy goldilocks boss says something insulting to me in her supposed French which I know is not French because she is not French and does not speak French.

And Johnny, who is trying to help me out, says, "Angela didn't write that poem about Mrs. Brinks! She wrote it about her dog!"

If you gave Nanette Manoir a real french fry at that moment she would not have been happier. "Oh, she did, did she?" Nanette says as she walks away with a nasty grin on her un-French face.

That's when Gina Lash and I know that not only am I dead but I am buried, too.

CHAPTER FIVE

Back in the classroom, Mrs. Brinks is still smiling at me like I am her favorite, which is what I have become. She makes me sit in the desk up front and moves Ninnie Wart to the back. I cannot even enjoy that moment because first of all, Nanette is not even mad, and second of all, Nanette is raising her hand. "Mrs. Brinks?" she says. "About Angela's lovely poem . . ."

Uh-oh, here it comes, I think. And I am right. When Ninny tells her who I have written my poem about, Mrs. Brinks not only turns as red as a fire engine, she screeches like one too. "HER DOG?" she screams. Then she starts looking at my poem as if it were a list of personal insults against her, and the whole class starts laughing and barking like dogs.

"Mrs. Brinks, I tried to tell you," I say.

"SILENCE!" Mrs. Brinks screams. Then she makes me take an eraser and erase the poem she once loved off the blackboard. As I am doing that I start wishing I had written a much shorter poem, because it feels like it is taking forever. "After you get rid of that abomination, Miss Anaconda," says Mrs. Brinks (she was not done with me yet), "I want you to go outside and clap every trace of chalk off those erasers!"

The only good part of that job (which I hate more than anything, by the way) is that I did not have to hear the world's biggest teacher's pet get up and read her French queen poem, which I knew would surely take forever.

As I was clapping those erasers and wishing I could redecorate Miss Ninnie Poo's fancy un-French dress, I started thinking up a new poem. . . .

What if Mrs. Brinks was none other than Queen Marie Antoinette herself, with a big white wig and her pet Nanette bowing before her? I thought to myself:

Oh, little Nin, I must proclaim,
Your poem about that queen was lame.
And you, Mrs. Brinks, with your head so big,
Your nose is running, and your hair is a wig!

And then what if when Mrs. Brinks blows her nose, her wig shoots up and lands sideways on her head? Then King and I would come in with crowns on our heads and we would take those horrible two to the land of their dreams!

Come Ninny and Brinksy to land in Paree,
Where my dog King and me
Make all the rules to which you must agree.
My dearest of teachers and your favorite pet,
Please don't you worry and, geez, don't you fret.

And then what if Uncle Nicky, who drives his red Corvette way too fast, pulls up and none other than Gina Lash steps out of the front seat carrying a tray of her all-time favorite Tiny Dottie snack cakes? Just as Brinks and Nin are going to the guillotine, of all places.

For here is Gina come to serve
You little cakes you don't deserve.
Oh, naughty, Nonnie, prissy miss

And Marie Antoi-Brinks, whose butt you kiss.
Let's see how you cackle when canine King tackles
The difficult chore—
You insufferable bores—
Of sentencing you
To a swirlie for two.

And then, just when they think their heads
will come off, Brinks and Nin instead realize
that they must suffer a fate worse than death:
Cleaning King's toilet!

"We beg you for mercy," you'll pathetically cry.
"Oh, greatest of queens, ten times smarter than I."
"But, Angela, save us!"
You'll snivel and snort.
"Don't be outrageous," I'll kindly retort.
Scrub little Ninnie, you too, Mrs. Brinks.
The King can't have germs
In the water she drinks.

And because poor Nanette hates scrubbing King's toilet so much, I can hear her screaming, "AAAAAAAH."

Just then I stop clapping my erasers and realize that Nanette Manoir really *is* screaming in real life for real. And she is standing right next to me. "SNAP OUT OF IT!" she screams. It is as if she can tell what I am thinking about.

"Mrs. Brinks sent me out to get you, but look at you now. You're all white, covered in that filthy chalk dust. You look like my DOG!"

"So sorry, Nanette, I was lost in a FOG."

You see, even though this was one of the most horrible days of my life, I still found out that poetry is kind of fun. And I also found out that I'm actually kinda good at it.

"Let's go back inside before the sun damages my fine silk ATTIRE," said Nanette.

"After you, Ninnie Poo, who I've always ADMIRED." I hate to admit it, but I was having fun outside with my poems and ideas. And since Nanette Manoir is the official teacher's pet, and because she said Mrs. Brinks wanted me inside, I figured I had to follow her. . . .

Oops, was that *my* chalk handprint on the back of Ninnie's favorite silk dress?

Story Number Two

THE SUBSTITUTE

CHAPTER ONE

It is no big surprise that breakfast is the worst meal of the day in my house where I live. Why? You might ask. Well, as much as I hate to give them any attention, my two dimwit brothers, Derek and Mark, take all the delicious candy fruit out of the fruity flakes cereal, leaving me with only the flakes, which you might as well buy as plain fruitless flakes because they are boring and have no taste. Derek and Mark (or "Dork" and

"Mork," as I like to call them) also take all the milk, which makes the plain cornflakes even more horrible and impossible to eat. Then Baby Lulu, who I secretly think is on the side of the dimwits, usually spills her bottle all over me *and* my homework, and I am just lucky I have my dog King to lick it up.

But what made this morning even more bad than ever was, I was supposed to think up what I was doing for my rain forest project and by the time I got finished fighting with my brothers and getting squirted by Baby Lulu, I did not. So when I got to my third-grade class at Tapwater Springs Elementary School, I expected my teacher, Mrs. Brinks, to get mad because I did not have a thought in my head about the rain forest, much less a project about the rain forest. But then, instead of things being really bad, all of a sudden things started to get really good.

First, when we got to our classroom, Mrs.

Brinks was not there, which was good sign number one. Then, the principal made an announcement and said that Mrs. Brinks was sick and we would be getting a substitute teacher.

As if you didn't know, the only one who was not cheering was Miss Do-Nothing Class Monitor Teacher's Pet Rat, Nanette Manoir, who had worn her endangered species crocodile shoes as a visual example of her rain forest subject. Then Johnny Abatti gets the idea to make paper airplanes out of our math homework, and guess what? Mine flew much better than his! A lot better. So good that it hit the lady with short hair and glasses who was coming into the room. Our substitute teacher. Oh, no, I am finished before she even starts, I thought to myself. But that's when really good thing number two happened.

"Anyone here named Angela?" she asked as she read my name off the math homework that was now a paper airplane.

"That's Angela, there!" said Johnny Abatti, who was not being mean or trying to get me in trouble like Ninnie Wart would, but who was just being Johnny, who is not that smart.

"Uh-oh," said Gina Lash, who is my best friend and who *is* very smart.

Instead of getting mad or making me go to the principal's office as Mrs. Brinks would if she got hit with my math homework (which was turned into a paper airplane), this lady fixed the wing on my plane and flew it right back to me! If only you could've seen the look on Nanette Manoir's un-French face and on the faces of her clone drone friends January and Karlene!

CHAPTER TWO

Then the substitute teacher said her name was Geraldine Klump. "But you can call me Geri." Like she was a friend of ours, like Johnny or Gina or Angela (me!). I don't know about you, but mostly when we have a substitute, our class does not listen, and instead of getting schoolwork done, we get nothing done. But that never stops Nanette Manoir from trying to be the goody-goody boss of all time.

"Miss Klump," said Nanette to Geri, not calling her Geri like she asked us to. "I feel it is my academic duty to go over our homework assignment from last night, and I am fully prepared to discuss the topic of my rain forest project, which is 'The Scandalous Shortage of the Crocodile.'"

"Endangered species, now that's a topic a girl could sink her teeth into," said Geri. Uh-oh, was she starting to make our little Na-nutski *her* pet too?

But I shouldn't have been so worried, because when Nanette explained to Geri that the theme of her project wasn't about the crocodiles themselves (which she didn't care about), but only that there were not enough crocodile pocketbooks or shoes in the world on account of the international trade bans, Geri got really mad. "Young lady," she said. "*That's* not a project. That's a peck full of poppycock!"

Was that Nanette Manoir she was talking to? No one in the class could believe it. Least of all, Nanette and her copycat twin Nins, January and Karlene.

"Do you think she's really a teacher?" asked Gina Lash. Because who ever heard of a substitute teacher you actually liked?

CHAPTER THREE

Later that day in the cafeteria I was a little jealous of Johnny and Gina because they each had thought of good rain forest projects. Gina was writing about "Amazon Crunch," that peanut and raisin mix you can buy at the grocery store, and Johnny was writing about cannibals. And even though I was not home getting milk spilled on me and having my cereal ruined by those caveman leftovers from the Stone Age, Derek and

Mark, I still could not think of a good enough project.

That's when good thing number three happened.

"Hey, Angela, is this seat taken?" It was Geri and she wanted to sit with us!

At first I was surprised. "Are you talking to me?" I asked. Teachers never know your name on the first day of teaching.

"Never forget a face full of freckles," she said as she sat down right next to me, Gina, and Johnny! And you know what? She told me she had freckles just like me when she was a kid!

"Yoo-hoo, Miss Klump! There's plenty of room over here at the popular kids' table!" said the voice of Nanette Manoir, which could kill a crocodile just by its horrible sound alone.

"Fine right here, Janet," said Geri with a wave of her hand like Nanette did not matter at all.

"Its *Nanette*!" corrected Little Nin. But

Geri did not care, she was too busy opening up the scary-looking sandwich that they call lunch at our school.

"Wish we had some pizza," said Geri. "I've had better meals cooked by headhunters."

"Wow!" said Johnny Abatti. "You know real, live headhunters?"

"Sure," said Geri. And she showed us pictures of herself in the actual rain forest with actual rain forest hunters with spears and necklaces made of teeth.

"Look at those houses the headhunters live in," I said. "They look exactly like the tree house Johnny and I built!"

"Hey, that's a great idea for your rain forest project!" Geri said, easy as pie. And she gave me the picture for me to keep. What a great day this was turning out to be—not only did I have a teacher who actually liked me and not Nanette Manoir, but I had a project to do that I actually wanted to do!

At home I decided that the only way my brother Derek could pay me back for ruining every breakfast of my entire life was to let me borrow his Popsicle stick collection to build my rain forest project. Of course I was not going to *tell* him that I was borrowing it because I knew he would never let me have it if I asked him for it.

After a messy start with King, the best dog in all the world, who got the sticks glued to her fur, and me, who got the sticks glued to my fingers, I built a real model of an actual headhunter's house. Just like in Geri's picture. I couldn't wait to take it to school the next day, where I knew everyone would be thrilled and amazed. The only thing left that my house needed was a roof of straw. The straw was not even a problem to get, because I was able to take it out of Scamp our pet hamster's cage and I'm sure he didn't even miss it.

CHAPTER FOUR

The next day in the schoolyard Gina Lash was the first one to get excited when I held up my model of my Amazon headhunter's house. "Just think," she said. "Someone ate all those Popsicles!"

"Just be careful not to touch it," I said. "It's still a little wet."

Now, I don't know what it is about Johnny Abatti, but sometimes he does exactly what you ask him not to do. And it's not because

he is mean like a certain baloney-headed girl I know, or because he can't hear so great or because he only uses half his brain. He is just being Johnny, but as soon as I said "don't touch it," Johnny goes and gets his finger stuck to my house. Things might've turned out fine, but before Gina Lash and I could figure out how to get Johnny's finger unstuck so that my house would be okay, Ninnie Wart and her dummy duet come strolling along to make sure that things would not turn out fine at all.

"EW!" said the Nannoying one. "A house of germs from Popsicle sticks that have been in other people's mouths! Let's get out of here. Coming, John?" As her putrid pals were yelling, "Gross!" Nanette yanked Johnny's arm and since he was still stuck to my house, it got smashed to smithereens.

"You've broken my stilt house that is now

completely ruined!" I was almost crying. "Now it looks like I didn't even *do* my project!"

"Don't worry, Angela," said Gina Lash. "Geri will let you fix it. It's not as if you have to take that mess to Mrs. Brinks."

"She'd throw *that* right in the garbage," said Johnny.

And I knew that they were right, so I was feeling a lot better when I went into the classroom.

Why is it that just when you are sure things are going to turn out good they always end up turning out worse than you ever thought possible? Why is it that Mrs. Brinks is not our substitute teacher and Geri is not our real teacher? Why is it that when I brought my broken house into class, which I was all set to fix, Mrs. Brinks was standing there and not Geri?

"Angela Anaconda, what is that mess you are dropping everywhere?" Mrs. Brinks asked.

"Oh, Mrs. Brinks," said the Dizzy Nanizzy. "Too bad the joyous occasion of your return has been marred by all this gluey debris!"

"That's not debris, that's my rain forest project," I tried to explain. But I knew Mrs. Brinks would never understand.

"Very funny, young lady," she said. "Now clean up this mess immediately!"

And that's how I ended up having to go to the janitor's closet to get a bucket of water and wishing I could mop the floor with Ninny Poo's golden baloney curls.

CHAPTER FIVE

As I was running the water I started thinking about the rain forest and how at first I didn't like the stupid homework project, and along came Geri and then I loved it and now I could care less if I ever heard the words "rain forest" again.

I could see Mrs. Brinks and her precious Nanette (which rhymes with pet) playing croquet in their crocodile shoes while I, Angela Anaconda, officially welcomed them to the real rain forest. The rain forest where it really rains. Then I would pound out all my messages on the drum, warning all my little native friends to seek higher ground in order to escape the torrential downpours.

But what's this? Who's sitting under their sun umbrella while the rain is pouring down all around them? Why, it's Little Nin and Mrs. Brinks, who do not speak drum, so they cannot understand my warning. They are too busy trying to speak French, which they don't really know, either. Then, as the river overflows, they try to get on the roof of their cabana but they can't. That's when they start to yell and plead with me.

"Angela, Angela, save us!" they will tell me. "This raging river is ruining our crocodile cha-cha shoes!" I, of course, have climbed up on the top of my drum and am waiting for my friends in high places to arrive. And then Geri, the

good teacher who knows the real rain forest, will swing in on a vine and carry me to a real amazon tree house made of authentic Popsicle sticks.

As we watch Mrs. Brinks and Nanette twirling and screaming down the river, we realize that there is not much we can do to save them. Their only hope is if the relatives of the crocodiles that they have used for shoes decide to help them. And as Mrs. Brinks and Nanette head straight for the most treacherous waterfall on earth, Geri and I realize our friends are in danger. We then heroically swing on vines and rescue them—the most endangered of all species—our friends the crocodiles. It is amazing, but at that point I can almost hear Mrs. Brinks screaming, "ANGELAAA!" as she goes over the waterfall.

Suddenly I can actually feel the water on my feet too. And I can clearly hear Mrs. Brinks screaming, "Have you gone completely hooey?" I must have been daydreaming, because as I look down I see I am completely flooding the floor in the janitor's closet by letting the water run over the sink.

"After you mop up this mess, take yourself straight to the principal's office!" screams Mrs. Brinks.

Just great, I think, what else can go wrong now? I thought yesterday would be a bad day at school and it was the best day ever. Today I came to school with a project I really liked, to see a teacher I really liked, and now I not only have a project that no one likes, but I have a teacher I really don't like, and who really doesn't like me because she loves Nanette Manoir better than anyone. And not only that, but now I am on my way to the principal's office, which only happens when you are in the biggest trouble.

Having a substitute teacher that we all liked (except for Nanoozy and her crowd) was a big surprise. Having Mrs. Brinks return to school today was another surprise. But going to the principal's office was the biggest surprise of all. As I was standing in the doorway, the big chair spun around and I was all set to get yelled at when I couldn't believe my eyes!

"Geri?!"

"Hello, Angela! Today I'm substituting for the principal, who's sick. Probably from eating that cafeteria food. Grab a chair! Whadya say we order a pizza for lunch?"

Geri, the only *teacher* who was ever nice to me, was now the only *principal* who was ever nice to me. Over pizza I told Geri all about the rain forest house I built out of Popsicle sticks and how I flooded the janitor's closet. She said she thought it

would be a good time to ask Mrs. Brinks and her perfect class monitor Annette to clean out the janitor's closet.

"It's Nanette," I said.

"Right," she winked. "And since Mrs. Brinks and Annette will be so busy today, how about we go join the rest of your class out on the playground for what's left of the day."

The End